D

11/05

A Note to Parents and Caregivers:

Read-it! Joke Books are for children who are moving ahead on the amazing road to reading. These fun books support the acquisition and extension of reading skills as well as a love of books.

Published by the same company that produces *Read-it!* Readers, these books introduce the question/answer and dialogue patterns that help children expand their thinking about language structure and book formats.

When sharing joke books with a child, read in short stretches. Pause often to talk about the meaning of the jokes. The question/answer and dialogue formats work well for this purpose and provide an opportunity to talk about the language and meaning of the jokes. Have the child turn the pages and point to the pictures and familiar words. When you read the jokes, have fun creating the voices of characters or emphasizing some important words. Be sure to reread favorite jokes.

There is no right or wrong way to share books with children. Find time to read with your child, and pass on the legacy of literacy.

Adria F. Klein, Ph.D.
Professor Emeritus
California State University
San Bernardino, California

Editor: Christianne Jones
Designer: Joe Anderson
Page Production: Melissa Kes
Art Director: Keith Griffin
Managing Editor: Catherine Neitge
The illustrations in this book were prepared digitally.

Picture Window Books
5115 Excelsior Boulevard
Suite 232
Minneapolis, MN 55416
877-845-8392
www.picturewindowbooks.com

Printed in the United States of America.

Library of Congress Cataloging-in-Publication Data
Ziegler, Mark, 1954-
Critter jitters : a book of animal jokes / written by Mark Ziegler;
illustrated by Anne Haberstroh.
p. cm.–(Read-it! joke books–supercharged!)
ISBN 1-4048-0967-8
1. Animals–Juvenile humor. 2. Riddles, Juvenile. I. Haberstroh, Anne.
II. Title. III. Series.

PN6231.A5Z54 2004
818'.602–dc22   2004018432

Critter Jitters

A Book of Animal Jokes

By Mark Ziegler • Illustrated by Anne Haberstroh

Reading Advisers:

Adria F. Klein, Ph.D.
Professor Emeritus, California State University
San Bernardino, California

Rosemou District

What kind of monkey flies
through the sky?

A hot-air baboon.

What did the judge say when the skunk was on trial?

"Odor in the court!"

Why don't leopards play hide-and-seek?

Because they're always spotted.

What sport do horses like to play?

Stable tennis.

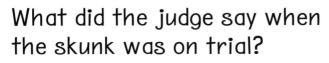

What do you give a pig who has a rash?

Oinkment.

What is worse than a centipede with sore feet?

A giraffe with a sore throat.

Why did the dog sit in the shade?

Because he didn't want to be a hot dog.

What is a bee's favorite treat?

Bumble gum.

What game do cows play
at parties?

Moosical chairs.

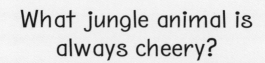

What jungle animal is always cheery?

A happy-potamus.

What do cows do on a date?

They go to the mooovies.

Why was the cow so good at math?

Because he always carried a cowculator.

Why did the cats get married?

Because they made a purrrfect match.

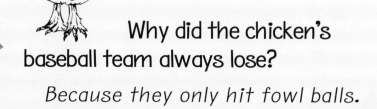

Why did the chicken's baseball team always lose?

Because they only hit fowl balls.

What do you call a crazy tick?

A looney-tick!

How do bees get to work?

They take the buzz.

What is a cat's favorite color?

Purrrple.

Did you hear about the kitten
that liked to play with string?

She had a ball.

Why was the bunny unhappy?

She was having a bad hare day.

How can you tell if a duck is broken?

It has a quack in it.

What do you get when you cross a dog with a hen?

Pooched eggs.

Where do dogs sleep when they're out in the woods?

In pup tents.

What did the oyster say when the police questioned it?

Nothing. He clammed up.

What books do skunks read?

Best smellers.

Where do dogs park their cars?

In barking lots.

What is a frog's favorite game?

Croak-kay.

Why wouldn't the elephant use a computer?

She was afraid of the mouse.

What shoes did the python wear when it went running?

Snakers.

What kind of computer did the crocodile buy?

One with lots of bytes.

What do you call a sleeping bull?

A bulldozer.

Why do birds fly south?

Because it's too far to walk.

Why did the crow sit on the telephone line?

He wanted to make a long-distance caw.

What sport do pigs play in the winter?

Ice hoggy.

What kind of dog can tell time?

A watchdog.

Why did the cow do jumping jacks?

She wanted to make milkshakes.

What do you call a flying skunk?

A smellicopter.

Why did the ram fall over the cliff?

He didn't see the ewe turn.

What is a duck's favorite snack?

Cheese and quackers.

Where do most lions live?

Mane Street.

What do you get when you cross
a snowball with a tiger?

Frostbite.

Did you hear the joke
about the skunk?

Yes. It really stunk!

Where do sheep get their hair cut?

At the Ba-Ba shop.

How do rabbits send letters?

By hare mail.

What do dogs eat at the movies?

Pupcorn.

What kind of dog likes to take a bath?

A shampoodle.

Read-it! Joke Books— Supercharged!

Beastly Laughs: A Book of Monster Jokes by Michael Dahl

Chalkboard Chuckles: A Book of Classroom Jokes by Mark Moore

Creepy Crawlers: A Book of Bug Jokes by Mark Moore

Critter Jitters: A Book of Animal Jokes by Mark Ziegler

Giggle Bubbles: A Book of Underwater Jokes by Mark Ziegler

Goofballs! A Book of Sports Jokes by Mark Ziegler

Lunchbox Laughs: A Book of Food Jokes by Mark Ziegler

Roaring with Laughter: A Book of Animal Jokes by Michael Dahl

School Kidders: A Book of School Jokes by Mark Ziegler

Sit! Stay! Laugh! A Book of Pet Jokes by Michael Dahl

Spooky Sillies: A Book of Ghost Jokes by Mark Moore

Wacky Wheelies: A Book of Transportation Jokes by Mark Ziegler

Looking for a specific title or level? A complete list
of *Read-it!* Readers is available on our Web site:
www.picturewindowbooks.com